The (Almost) True Story of Hope Winter
Persephone Litchfield

Dedications

To Ahlani Santos, Katrina Wirtz and Amaya Patterson, for letting me be who I am, and lighting up my world every day. You inspire me every day to be a better version of myself.

To Ellie Gift for following me into each story, and radiating positivity when writing was too much.

To Ella Lounds, who gave this story a second chance, and who has supported me through every bad draft, and helped me create good ones. You have made me a better writer, creator, and person.

To the actors and creatives who breathed life into this story.

And lastly,

To everyone that supported my ideas when this story was nothing but a seedling, and the people who helped give it the love it needed to grow. You are all the start of me, and I owe you more than I will ever have.

The (Almost) True Story of Hope Winter

Setting

Richmond, Oregon. 2015.

Characters

In order of appearance

YOUNG HOPE - A younger version of Hope. **8-12 F**

HOPE WINTER- A freshman in highschool, and a talented writer. **14-15 F**

CYNTHIA LABELLE - A sophomore in highschool, and a hopeful writer. **15-16 F**

BREE FLANDEL - A junior in highschool, and a writer. **17 F**

LIZ MARTIN - A junior in highschool, and an avid writer. **16-17 F**

ALLY COLCONE - A junior in high school, and a writer. **16-17 F**

PIERRE - A high school teacher, responsible for journalism. **M 30+**

JAYDIN PALLET - A sophomore in highschool, and an optimistic writer. **15-16 N/B**

WAVERLY - A Journalism student **16-17 F**

JOHN WOLLONS - A senior in high school, and Bree's ex. **17-18 M**

Ensemble - A group of co-ed students who speak on and off stage **14-18 M F N/B**
Speaking Ensemble: BOY 1, BOY 2, GIRL 1, GIRL 2, REAGAN, PRESTON

Act 1

Scene 1

YOUNG HOPE runs out, centerstage.

YOUNG HOPE: I can't wait. The people, the classes, the music! I can almost feel it! I'll be cool! People- they'll like me! And- I'll wear pretty dresses, and dance with cute boys. Once I make it to high school, I'll be popular! I'll go to parties. High school is going to be perfect. *Everything* will be perfect. I can hardly wait.

Lights fade out. Black stage. Overlapping offstage voices are heard.

O/S BOY 1: Sad to see the summer go.

O/S GIRL 1: Missing my summer nights already.

O/S BOY 1: First day of freshman!

O/S GIRL 1: Sophomore!

O/S BOY 2: Junior!

O/S GIRL 2: Senior year!

O/S GIRL 1: First day of school hashtag O O T D.

O/S BOY 1: Anyone have Gavinson for Geometry?

O/S GIRL 2: Nova Hills High School, I'm coming

ALL: First day of school!

The lights rise on HOPE standing center stage, but now surrounded by her bedroom. She wrings her hands, pacing.

HOPE: They're just teenagers, they're only teenagers. I need so much from today, and I just- I don't know. I'm scared. I thought I'd be cool, and popular. I mean, what if the other kids don't like me.

HOPE walks to her bed, where an outfit is laid out. She holds the shirt up to herself.

HOPE: I can't pull this off. *(She looks at it again) I* can't pull this off at *all.*

She runs to her offstage closet, throwing clothes onstage, sifting for a new top.

HOPE: I hate everything I have. I have nothing. No clothes.

HOPE sits on the side of the stage in her pajamas.

HOPE: My first day is already ruined. The most important day of my life is *ruined* and it's only- it's only-

HOPE gets up to grab her phone from her bed. She picks it up, horrified.

HOPE: 7:30?! Oh god, oh god, oh god.

HOPE runs to her overstuffed backpack and rummages through it.

HOPE: Notebooks? Yes. Pencils? Yes. Pens? Yes. Binder? Yes. Extra binder in case the first one gets full? Yes. *(She pauses).* I'll put some perfume in there in case I need it.

HOPE grabs a bottle off of her dresser and walks to her bag. She turns back to the dresser.

HOPE: What if my makeup wears off? I should probably bring my makeup bag with me.

HOPE grabs her makeup bag off of her dresser. She goes back to her backpack, but turns around to grab deodorant, a necklace, and a bottle of lotion as well. She places them in the backpack.

HOPE: Just in case I... need them.

HOPE struggles to zip her backpack but eventually gets it zipped. An offstage voice calls.

O/S VOICE: Are you ready for school?

HOPE: No, no, no, no-

HOPE runs offstage to get dressed. In HOPE's panic, YOUNG HOPE stands on the side of the stage.

YOUNG HOPE: I'll be so cute! Everyone will like me! I'll make friends, and we'll go to the mall, and I'll get to-

Hope O/S: I can't believe this is happening. Please don't let me be late.

YOUNG HOPE: I get to be the "It" girl. I'll be noticed.

Hope O/S: Everyone is going to stare at me! What kind of person is late on the first day.

YOUNG HOPE: Everyone will want to be me! Everyone will love me!

HOPE O/S: My teachers are going to hate me. I'm going to look lazy and unprepared and-

YOUNG HOPE: Reckless and wild and free! I'll wear clothes that are fun and exciting and-

HOPE walks out in a mundane outfit but begins to panic.

HOPE: Crazy. I look crazy.

O/S VOICE: Hope! Are you ready?!

HOPE: *(Calling offstage)* Uh- Yeah! Yeah, I'm coming!

HOPE takes a deep breath and walks offstage. She runs back, grabs her backpack and runs back off.

Blackout

Scene 2

HOPE enters a classroom at Nova Hills High School. She looks around at the open desks. She walks towards a desk. GIRL 1 shakes her head.

GIRL 1: Sorry, I'm saving this for my friend.

HOPE wrings her hands and walks toward another empty desk. GIRL 2 shoots her a look. She stares at the floor. She walks towards the back, still wringing her hands. CYNTHIA speaks, sitting in a desk.

CYNTHIA: Hey!

HOPE turns towards CYNTHIA and points to herself.

CYNTHIA: Yeah, you! Do you need a seat?

HOPE: Yeah, I'm not sure where to-

CYNTHIA gestures to the seat next to her. HOPE sits.

HOPE: Thank you.

CYNTHIA: No problem.

HOPE: I'm Hope.

CYNTHIA: Nice to meet you, Hope, I'm Cynthia.

HOPE shakes CYNTHIA's hand.

CYNTHIA: Okay, this sounds mean, and I don't mean it that way, but you seem new.

HOPE: Yeah, I'm a freshman.

CYNTHIA: You're a freshman? Are you sure you're in *this* class?

HOPE pulls out her schedule and shows it to CYNTHIA.

CYNTHIA: Honors Physics with Roberton…huh, I guess you are in this class.

HOPE: Are freshmen not usually in physics?

CYNTHIA: Not usually, no. This is mostly juniors and seniors.

HOPE: Oh, I didn't know.

CYNTHIA: It's okay! It's not like you're not allowed. Anyway, we can be early birds together.

HOPE: You're a freshman?

CYNTHIA: I'm a sophomore, but my mom just insists I take the most advanced classes I can. What's your excuse?

HOPE: Oh, I was in this other school, in Bend, but it was this pretentious private school. So, when I moved to Richland, I found out that I'm ahead in most of my classes.

CYNTHIA: Oh, that's great!

HOPE: I guess!

CYNTHIA: Tons of freshman would *kill* to skip the boring classes, you got lucky.

HOPE: Nice to know. *(Beat.)* Dumb question, where *is* Miss Roberton?

BOY 1 pipes up from the back, speaking to HOPE but also to the classroom.

BOY 1: If she's not here after fifteen minutes we're legally allowed to leave.

A chorus of students chime in in agreement. CYNTHIA rolls her eyes.

CYNTHIA: I have no idea. She teaches a ton of classes, so sometimes she runs late.

HOPE: Oh, gotcha.

CYNTHIA: Yeah. So how are you liking Nova Hills?

HOPE: It's...big.

CYNTHIA: Yeah, a lot of space for a lot of students.

HOPE: Do you ever get used to it?

CYNTHIA: Oh, don't worry about it, you'll be able to navigate your schedule blind in a week or two. What else are you taking?

HOPE glances down at her schedule.

HOPE: Algebra two, English three.

CYNTHIA: *Three?!*

HOPE: English is kind of my thing. I was ahead in Bend, so I'm way ahead here.

CYNTHIA: Jeez. Okay, what else?

HOPE: Journalism and Latin.

CYNTHIA: Wow. What lunch do you have?

HOPE: I'm sorry?

CYNTHIA: There's a ton of kids here, so there's different lunches. I'm in C, it should be on your schedule.

HOPE: *(Looking through her schedule)* Uh, Lunch C!

CYNTHIA: No way! What are the odds.

Both: *(Jokingly)* One in Three!

They both laugh.

CYNTHIA: Well, you're more than welcome to sit with me, if you want to.

HOPE: Uh- yeah! How do I find you with all of these...people...everywhere?

CYNTHIA: Don't worry about it. English 3 is right next to my French class, so I can drop by and show you how to get to the cafeteria.

HOPE: That would be so helpful. Thank you, Cynthia.

CYNTHIA: Of course! You have to find a good group freshman year, nobody should have to go alone.

HOPE: That's really comforting.

CYNTHIA: Thanks!

The door opens as the teacher walks in, the students groan. CYNTHIA and HOPE turn forward to look at the front of the room and the teacher. HOPE smiles to herself.

Blackout

Scene 3

The cafeteria. BREE, LIZ, and ALLY sit together talking. BREE looks tired and rough, LIZ looks stressed out but put together, and ALLY seems to be overcompensating.

LIZ: Bree, I don't know what we could even do. I think Emma transferring to Boltly High really ended our chance at Writers' Circuit.

BREE: Is there *any* way we could find someone else? If we win, I'm so much closer to getting the scholarship I need for college.

LIZ: All the people who wanted to participate have their groups, and no offense, but I'm pretty sure nobody is dying to spend their fall slaving over a novella.

ALLY: There's tons of English nerds in this school, Liz.

LIZ: Correction. Nobody wants to spend their fall writing a novella with *us*.

ALLY: Are we really that bad?

LIZ: No offense, but everyone thinks we're exclusive and rude.

BREE: Nobody thinks that.

LIZ: Everyone thinks that.

BREE: There has to be some way.

ALLY: Just give it up, Bree. Emma left. Our shot at Writers' Circuit is over. Find another scholarship.

BREE: I am, but I haven't gotten accepted for any, Ally. That's not my fault.

LIZ: Don't you have like- straight As? That has to be worth something.

BREE: They just don't accept me, okay!

ALLY: Sorry.

LIZ: I didn't realize it was a sensitive subject, I'm sorry.

They sit in silence for a moment.

BREE: We have to find someone for Writers' Circuit. We need a fourth person.

ALLY: Can you just ask them to make an exception?

LIZ: The rules say no exceptions. You need four people in your writing team to compete.

BREE: Couldn't we just ask Emma to work with us online?

LIZ: She doesn't go to Nova Hills anymore. You have to be represented by your school.

ALLY: So, we're screwed.

BREE: We can find a way.

ALLY: And if we can't?

BREE: We will. We have to.

LIZ: Bree, please don't think your college education rides on Writers' Circuit.

BREE: It does!

LIZ: There will be other opportunities, I swear.

BREE: Liz, I'm a junior now. I don't have enough time to hope that money will appear out of nowhere. We need to find someone.

ALLY: Where would we find someone, Bree? Riddle me that.

BREE: We will. I know it.

ALLY sighs and shakes her head. The lights fade and rise up on HOPE and CYNTHIA at a table during lunch, mid-conversation.

CYNTHIA: You're a writer?

HOPE: I mean, nothing crazy, but yeah. I like it.

CYNTHIA: Books? Songs? Poems?

HOPE: Poems. I'm really big into sonnets right now.

CYNTHIA: Sonnets? Wow.

HOPE: I told you I went to a pretentious private school. I just-

CYNTHIA: No, I wasn't meaning to be patronizing I just- I don't hear a lot of sonnets. At least outside of Shakespeare.

HOPE: That's why I love them! They're gorgeous and ancient, and original. Nobody's doing them, but modern sonnets are just- gorgeous.

CYNTHIA: That's so cool, Hope. Like, honestly? That's awesome.

HOPE smiles kindly and pushes a hair behind her ear.

CYNTHIA: Are you? Blushing?

HOPE: Oh, I just- I'm not used to people letting me talk about these things, even less liking them.

CYNTHIA: Maybe you need some different people.

HOPE: That's the cool thing about moving. *(Beat.)* Everything's... different.

CYNTHIA: Oh, I'm sorry. I didn't want to-

HOPE: No, no it's okay. I didn't like the people back home anyway. They weren't very great friends.

CYNTHIA: Do you miss it?

HOPE: Bend? Yeah. I love the town. It's sweet, and simple. It's my home. But I think I'm willing to give Richmond a shot. I'm open to a new story.

CYNTHIA: That's admirable. I don't know what I'd do if I had to leave Richmond.

HOPE: Thanks.

CYNTHIA: I think you'll fit in pretty great here, for what it's worth.

HOPE: It's worth a lot. Thank you, Cynthia.

The bell rings. The girls get up and head out.
Blackout

Scene 4

HOPE sits at a desk in her journalism class. The classroom quickly fills up with students, including WAVERLY, JAYDIN and LIZ.

PIERRE: Welcome to Journalism, everyone! I'm seeing a lot of familiar faces. *(She gestures to students).* Matthew, Regan, Liz, Waverly, Jaydin. It's nice to see you all. But I'm also thrilled to see some fresh faces in the mix. I'm thrilled to welcome you to our Journalism program. I'll skip the monologuing, feel free to refer to the syllabus on your online classroom homepage. I'd prefer to keep the unnecessary work out of the classroom. So, without further ado, let's dive right in!

The class nods vaguely

PIERRE: The main task of the Journalism program is writing for the Warrior Weekly. However, that is reserved for our top journalists. The rest of you will spend your time learning how to write as eloquently and efficiently as possible. I'll leave the dramatics out, the people writing for warrior weekly are Regan Thomas, Preston Jacobs, Waverly Jones, Jaydin Pallet, Liz Smith, and Hope Winter.

The people that were called and a few others look at HOPE with confusion. HOPE sinks into her seat. PIERRE takes notice.

PIERRE: Now, I know Hope is new. But she has earned her spot-on Warrior Weekly. She has talent and is a valuable contribution to the newspaper team. Just because she is a freshman does not mean-

A toned-down outburst of students respond

STUDENTS: A *freshman?!*

PIERRE: The rules do not prohibit freshman from being on the Warrior Weekly staff, only that upperclassmen receive priority. I expect professionalism from you all.

The students calm down.

PIERRE: Warrior Weekly staff, follow Waverly to the Newspaper room.

WAVERLY leads everyone to a new room, where they all sit around in a circle.

WAVERLY: So, I know most of you. But just to refresh, get everything in on time, be professional, and write well and we'll be on good terms. We need to start coming up with Friday's article. Pierre wants us to have a paper out asap, start off the year with a bang.

JAYDIN: So, you want us to come up with a good topic *on the spot*?

WAVERLY: I know, Jaydin, but it's really not up to me.

REAGAN: What are we going to write about? This is literally the first day of school?

WAVERLY: Back to school advice?

PRESTON: Right, because that sets a tone for a hard-hitting student paper.

WAVERLY: There's nothing hard hitting to talk about! It's the first day!

LIZ: Cafeteria lunches?

REAGAN: Basic.

JAYDIN: Teacher scandals?

PRESTON: And get yourself suspended?

HOPE: Does it have to be an article?

Everyone looks at HOPE, and all but LIZ and JAYDIN cock their eyebrows.

WAVERLY: Elaborate.

HOPE: Sure, there's no time to write an article for the paper, but why start with an article? Start with a poem. Short, sweet, and different. Make it real and attention grabbing.

WAVERLY: You want us to put a poem for our kickoff piece?

HOPE: Think about it, it's expressive, it's new, and it's unexpected!

Everyone nods in agreement, slightly surprised that HOPE had the good idea.

WAVERLY: Who wants to write it?

LIZ: How about we all contribute some ideas and then pick our favorite.

WAVERLY: Okay. Everyone, give us your best back to school poem.

Everyone begins talking, and HOPE stays silent, writing in her notebook

REAGAN: School is very fun, for the students who come here, Nova Hills high school

WAVERLY: A *good* poem

PRESTON: Touché

LIZ: School is a scary place, but we'll help you handle it with grace

WAVERLY: Ooo, I like that, keep it going.

JAYDIN: Bullies won't hit your face, or call you a disgrace

WAVERLY: And we lost it.

HOPE puts her notebook on the table and reads aloud

HOPE: *(Reading)* When the high tides roll over your pen
And you feel like you're stuck in past time
Asking how, why, if, where and when
This mountain got harder to climb

Remember we always stand here
Your friendly school newspaper friends
So that when you feel high school's unclear
Your answers do not have an end

When the football team misses a catch
Or the school board announces new funds
Information is never a stretch
And getting informed always feels fun

So, trust us your Warrior Weekly
To deliver your news completely

HOPE pulls her notebook back into her lap and closes it. The rest of the team looks at her and shrugs and nods.

WAVERLY: I mean it's not perfect, but I guess it's good enough.

JAYDIN: Is that what we're using?

WAVERLY: Yeah, it's better than anything else we've got.

LIZ: Great!

PRESTON: Are we done then?

WAVERLY: I mean, I guess we are but-

REAGAN takes off, followed by PRESTON.

JAYDIN: Nice poem, Hope. Sounded great.

HOPE giggles

HOPE: Thank you.

JAYDIN exits. WAVERLY collects her things and leaves. HOPE gets up to exit, but LIZ stops her.

LIZ: I liked your sonnet.

HOPE: Thanks. I mean- it's not really a sonnet because of the syllables, though.

LIZ: Oh, I liked your poem then. You must be pretty great to be a freshman and in Journalism. Much less the Warrior Weekly staff.

HOPE: I just like writing.

LIZ: Look, I know that this sounds really weird, but just hear me out.

HOPE: Uh…. okay?

LIZ: So, my friends, Bree, Ally, and I were planning on competing in this competition called the Writers' Circuit.

HOPE: Writers' Circuit?

LIZ: It's this thing where you team up with three other people and write. If you win it's a huge deal. It looks great on college applications, you can get scholarships. It's huge.

HOPE: Okay.

LIZ: So, my friends and I had four people, but one of us got transferred. Now, we only have three on our team, so we can't compete.

HOPE: So…

LIZ: So… I was wondering if you'd join our team.

HOPE: I'd just have to write?

LIZ: Well, write and work with your team but yeah, just write and edit.

HOPE: I'd love to!

LIZ: Really?!

HOPE: Yeah! That sounds like a ton of fun.

LIZ: It means the world to me, and my friends. If I texted you the address, would you be okay coming to my house to work with my friends and I on our story?

HOPE: When?

LIZ: Like, tonight.

HOPE: Wow, that's fast...

LIZ: Yeah, we're running behind.

HOPE: I'll talk to my mom and make it work. Should I give you my number?

LIZ: Oh, yeah, sorry!

HOPE hands LIZ her phone, and LIZ enters HOPE's number into her phone.

LIZ: See you tonight!

HOPE: See ya!

Blackout

Scene 5

BREE, LIZ, ALLY, and HOPE sit in LIZ's room. They all talk, except for HOPE who looks out of place.

LIZ: Is he still into you, what's going on with that?

BREE: I don't know, who cares, he's *wild.*

ALLY: Just avoid him.

BREE: I don't care...about him.

ALLY: Whatever you say.

BREE: We should write about him.

ALLY: About John?

BREE: *(giggling)* Yeah.

ALLY: Right because I'm sure writing about your ex would go over *so* well.

LIZ: Speaking of which, what *are* we writing about.

HOPE: I was actually just thinking about it! I love sonnets, and I was thinking we could write a series of-

ALLY: Writers' Circuit is for novellas only.

HOPE: I thought you just had to write...

LIZ: Sorry, I didn't mean to give you that impression.

HOPE: No, it's okay. Novellas are fun too, I guess!

ALLY: I think we should write it from the perspective of a girl contemplating suicide and it's all diary entries but-

BREE: Ally... take a breath. Lay off the edge, okay.

LIZ: What about fantasy? It's never popular in Writers' Circuit. We could world build. Maybe fairies?

HOPE: What about a fairy/mermaid love story?

LIZ: Where they can only meet on shore!

ALLY: And one day, the beach is destroyed by a disaster, and they lose touch.

HOPE: And they have to find each other again!

ALLY: No! Happy endings are cliché. I want something *real.*

HOPE: Okay...

LIZ: What about historical fiction?

HOPE: Like Victorian England?

ALLY: And the plague?

    HOPE and LIZ sigh, BREE giggles again

BREE: Ally, stop.

ALLY: Sadness sells!

LIZ: I don't want to contribute to all the depressing media. I want to write something positive.

ALLY: Positivity is coddling.

HOPE: How about a compromise!

LIZ: What would you suggest?

HOPE: What about a dark story with a happy ending.

ALLY: No happy endings.

HOPE: Fine, a happy story with a sad ending.

ALLY: I can live with that.

BREE: *(Still giggling)* Can you really?

LIZ: I liked the fairy falling for a mermaid idea. It's fun and cliché, and a dark twist could make it original.

HOPE: Then fairy/mermaid love story it is.

BREE: Crazy.

LIZ: Bree, what's up with you.

BREE: Hmmm?

ALLY: Earth to Bree? What's up with you?

BREE: Oh, c'mon, Ally. Don't be such a buzzkill.

> *LIZ and ALLY exchange looks.*

LIZ: Are you high?

BREE: Pshh no!

ALLY: Bree…

BREE: Get off of my back!

LIZ: Bree, talk to me.

> *BREE looks LIZ in the eyes*

BREE: What?

LIZ: Are you high?

BREE: A little

ALLY: Jeez, Bree. You gotta stop doing this whenever we hang out.

BREE: If you want some, we could do it together-

ALLY: That's not what I meant.

BREE: I'm just having fun.

ALLY: What if my dad smells weed on me? I'm around you *all* the time.

LIZ: This can't be good for you.

BREE: It's just weed.

HOPE: Still.

ALLY: Still!

BREE: Chill, guys. I'm okay.

LIZ: Just...Just be careful I guess.

HOPE wrings her hands. She distances herself from BREE and stares at the floor. ALLY rolls her eyes at the conversation and starts a new one.

ALLY: Anyway, about John.

Blackout

Scene 6

The cafeteria. CYNTHIA sits at a table, and HOPE comes to join her.

HOPE: Hey!

CYNTHIA: Hey! How did the rest of your first day go?

HOPE: Good, hectic. I made some friends, a lot happened. Yours?

CYNTHIA: Good, can't say I'd describe mine as hectic, or particularly eventful.

HOPE: I'm sorry.

CYNTHIA: Don't be, I wasn't sad about it. I know the stressful part is yet to come.

HOPE laughs lightly

CYNTHIA: So, what made your day hectic yesterday?

HOPE: Well, I got put on the newspaper staff, and-

CYNTHIA: Wait, what?!

HOPE: I know. I didn't know it was special. I don't get it but it's okay. Anyway, I suggested this poem for the newspaper, and I guess they liked it, but mostly Liz.

CYNTHIA: Liz Martin?

HOPE: I guess? Do you know her?

CYNTHIA: I've talked to her here and there.

HOPE: Well she asked me to join her team for their writing competition, uh, Writers' Circuit. It sounded like fun, so I said yes. By the end of the night, I was at her house with two other girls.

CYNTHIA: Ally and Bree?

HOPE: How'd you know?

CYNTHIA: They're all attached at the hip. They've been friends since Kindergarten.

HOPE: Go figure!

CYNTHIA: Yeah. They're not very nice to the people not sewn into their little group, I mean they're not evil, or bullies, or anything. They're just...I don't know. Kind of petty, they're mean to people if they cross them, I'm just saying that they tend to be hostile to people that aren't close to them.

HOPE: Oh…

CYNTHIA: No, don't let that scare you! They're just a little...cold. This could be a great opportunity for you to pursue your passion.

HOPE: Well, not really.

CYNTHIA: What do you mean?

HOPE: I thought we just had to write *something*. I didn't find out until later that it had to be a novella. I don't really know how to write a story. I know how to write poems.

CYNTHIA: Are you going to drop their group?

HOPE: No. It seemed really important to them, and I don't want to let them down. Also, who knows. Maybe a novella would be a good way to learn and branch out.

CYNTHIA: Sounds great! Versatility is great!

HOPE: Thanks. What about you? Besides the first day of school, what's up with you?

CYNTHIA: Well, my summer vocal showcase on Friday! I'm so excited!

HOPE: Vocal showcase?

CYNTHIA: Yeah! My choir has this performance where everyone gets to sing a solo or duet. It's really fun and I love my song! I think both my parents are going to come and my friends too!

HOPE: That sounds so fun!

CYNTHIA: Right?! You could come if you wanted to. I'd love it if you did!

HOPE: I'd love to come!

CYNTHIA: Oh my god, thank you! I'll get you tickets and everything! I'm so excited!

HOPE: I am too! It'll be an honor to watch you perform!

Blackout

Scene 7

Journalism class. PIERRE stands up front. All the journalism students except for LIZ are in the classroom.

PIERRE: Today, we're going to start a group project. You'll be put in groups of three. The object of this assignment is to find an issue in our school and write an article on it and your personal solution. The project is due in three days, so use your time wisely.

As PIERRE assigns groups, they meet up and find a corner or area of the stage.

PIERRE: Waverly, Mark, and Regan. Tristen, Abraham, and Krysta. Sophia, Marcus and Ella. And Liz, Hope, and Jaydin.

JAYDIN and HOPE meet at desks in the center.

JAYDIN: Do you know where Liz is?

HOPE: No, you?

JAYDIN: No. *(Beat.)* Well, I guess it's just us then.

HOPE: I guess so.

JAYDIN: So, in the whole day and a half you've been here, what jarring problems have you noticed?

They laugh

HOPE: Oh, the hallways are too loud.

JAYDIN: Oh?

HOPE: And the school is too big.

JAYDIN: Is it now?

HOPE: Oh, and the cafeteria?

JAYDIN: Do tell.

HOPE: Needs to be mopped.

JAYDIN: Perfect. I think you just nailed our expose down.

HOPE: It writes itself.

JAYDIN: Big, loud school needs to be mopped.

HOPE: That's a terrible title.

JAYDIN: And you have a better one?

HOPE: "You'll need a bigger mop for this job" says Nova Hills High School.

JAYDIN: You left out the loud.

HOPE: All caps.

They laugh

JAYDIN: That is a very tempting title.

HOPE: The only way to get rid of temptation is to yield it.

JAYDIN: Really?

HOPE: What?

JAYDIN: You're an Oscar Wilde girl?

HOPE: I'm more of a William Wordsworth girl, but the Wilde quote fit better.

JAYDIN: Wordsworth. I should've guessed.

HOPE: Based off of what?

JAYDIN: Your poem for Weekly Warrior was a sonnet.

HOPE: I mean it wasn't really a- I mean- lots of poets write sonnets.

JAYDIN: You keep telling yourself that.

HOPE playfully furrows her brow, then laughs.

HOPE: Who's your favorite?

JAYDIN: John Keats.

HOPE: A thing of beauty is a joy forever.

JAYDIN: You know your poets.

HOPE: I try to know a lot about things people don't much care about.

JAYDIN: That sounds like a good way to live.

HOPE: I would hope so.

JAYDIN: *(little laugh) Hope* so. Like your name-

HOPE shakes her head

HOPE: Least original joke in the world. No.

JAYDIN: My comedy career is over.

HOPE: It never began

JAYDIN: Oh boo. Not even funny.

They laugh.

HOPE: We should work on this project.

JAYDIN: Well, we have our title, so there's a start.

Blackout

Scene 8

LIZ and BREE sit in BREE's room, which seems slightly run down. LIZ sits in a chair, annotating a book. BREE looks thinner and washed out, BREE sits at an older computer, typing. They talk while they work.

BREE: *(Reading from her computer)* In the end, are we not all Nora? All trapped in our own tarantella, dancing until we drop. *(She looks up)* Good?

LIZ: Honest answer?

BREE: That's why I read it to you.

LIZ: No.

BREE: Oh c'mon! Why not!

LIZ: First off, you used "we", "our", and "my" about forty times.

BREE: Oh, I forgot about that.

LIZ: Secondly, your conclusion comes off pretentious and off-putting.

BREE: Yikes.

LIZ: Also, the entire paper says that Nora's tarantella was what killed her. That's not what the tarantella means, and it makes you look like you didn't read the book.

BREE: Oh.

LIZ: You did...read the book, right?

BREE: Yeah, of course!

LIZ looks at BREE for a moment.

BREE: Okay, fine, I just got busy.

LIZ: You love reading, was this one just not your speed?

BREE: I was just too busy with Writers' Circuit.

LIZ: Bree, are you kidding? You haven't written *anything* for Writers' Circuit.

BREE: Well, we had to scrap everything when you and Hope came up with the unicorn love story.

LIZ: It's a fairy and a mermaid. The story is about a fairy and a mermaid.

BREE: Same difference.

LIZ: What's going on with you? Is it John?

BREE: No, it's not John. I don't care about John.

LIZ: Then what? You're not only acting strange but now you're just skipping assignments?!

BREE: Liz, I think you're blowing things out of proportion.

LIZ: Am I?

BREE: Yes! It's one assignment. One.

LIZ: You're just… you've changed, Bree.

BREE: People have a tendency to do that.

LIZ stares at BREE for a moment. LIZ shakes her head and goes back to her book.

LIZ: I'm sorry I even brought it up.

BREE: No, it's…

LIZ: You're right. It's just an assignment.

BREE turns back around too.

BREE: How *is* the Writers' Circuit story coming along?

LIZ: Shouldn't you know? You're the one who said you needed it so badly.

BREE: Liz!

LIZ: Sorry.

Awkward pause. They both look at their individual tasks. LIZ looks back up at BREE.

LIZ: A fairy named Rosa finds a mermaid named Sylvia in the forest, moments away from suffocating. Rosa gets her to water and helps her find her way back home. On the way, they fall in love.

BREE: Cliché.

LIZ: I liked it.

BREE: I didn't say cliché was a bad thing, Liz.

LIZ: Oh.

They smile at each other.

LIZ: Your room is freezing.

BREE: You said that when you came in.

LIZ: I know, but I thought it would warm up.

BREE: It doesn't.

LIZ: Can you turn on the heat?

BREE: No.

LIZ: Why not? It's cold. I'm sure your mom won't flip out if you turn on the heat, I mean-

BREE: We don't have any.

LIZ: What?

BREE: We can't heat the house.

LIZ: Why?!

BREE: My mom got laid off, and she got severance pay but-

LIZ: You said your mom was at work.

BREE: She is, well- She's in Washington looking for a new job.

LIZ: *Washington?!* You're moving?

BREE: No, she hasn't gotten a job there, and if she did I'd stay with my grandma.

LIZ: Why don't you just stay with her now?

BREE: Liz, it's just- it's complicated.

> *Silence. LIZ takes a moment and asks with a lighter tone.*

LIZ: Can I borrow a jacket?

BREE: Yeah, of course.

> *BREE walks to her closets and rummages through. She pulls out a jacket and hands it to LIZ, who recoils as she grabs it.*

BREE: You alright there?

LIZ: Do you not-?

LIZ puts her nose to the jacket and smells it.

LIZ: Do you not smell this?

BREE: I wear deodorant, Liz.

LIZ: Bree, I'm serious. It reeks of-

LIZ puts her nose to the jacket and smells it again.

LIZ: It smells like vinegar. Like weed and vinegar.

BREE's eyes widen, she arches her back and stiffens defensively.

BREE: Are you going to lecture me about smoking? It's just weed, Liz.

LIZ: First of all, you're 17, second of all, weed doesn't smell like vinegar.

BREE: How would you know what weed smells like?

LIZ: Because I'm around you all the time.

BREE: Oh my god, Liz. Really?

LIZ: Bree, just explain. I'm jumping to worst case scenarios here, just tell me the truth.

BREE: And what's your worst-case scenario then?

LIZ: *Heroin*, Bree! I'm waiting for you to tell me you're not doing heroin.

BREE looks at LIZ blankly.

LIZ: Please tell me you're not doing heroin.

BREE: I'm- I'm not doing heroin.

LIZ: I want to believe you-

BREE: You said to tell you I'm not doing heroin! Why are you mad that I'm not?!

LIZ: Just tell me the truth.

BREE: I'm telling you the truth.

>   *LIZ looks at BREE, hurt and confused. She exits.*
>
>   **Blackout.**

Scene 9

The library. JAYDIN and HOPE sit together, working on their project. They laugh as they talked, obviously having fun.

JAYDIN: Okay but hear me out. When water touches something, it's wet.

HOPE: Water is always touching water; therefore, water is not wet.

JAYDIN: You're not listening!

HOPE: I'm 100% listening!

HOPE tucks her hair behind her ear.

JAYDIN: I'm not going to get anywhere with this am I?

HOPE: I don't think so.

JAYDIN: Then we should just focus on the project, I guess?

HOPE goes frantic, trying to keep JAYDIN'S attention.

HOPE: I mean, yeah, I guess! If you're lame!

JAYDIN tilts their head and furrows their brow.

HOPE: No, oh god, I was kidding, I just…

She opens her binder.

HOPE: I didn't mean to be like…anyway-uh, I was looking at the numbers for Nova Hills High and our class sizes are 2.4 times the size of the national average.

JAYDIN: And?

HOPE: It's an easy topic. Big class sizes mean our education is less personal. If our education is less personal then-

JAYDIN: We do worse.

HOPE: Exactly. Easy thesis.

JAYDIN: Easy A. So where do we start the paper?

HOPE: Well, I was thinking we could-

LIZ and ALLY enter, cutting HOPE off.

LIZ: Hey!

HOPE: Hey! Where've you been?

LIZ: What?

HOPE: Journalism. You missed journalism yesterday and today.

LIZ: Oh, I had to help with some stuff for student council.

HOPE: You're in student council?

LIZ: Yeah. Pierre said I could drop the project.

HOPE: Oh!

LIZ: Sorry, I should've called.

JAYDIN: It's really no problem. We have our project all laid out.

LIZ: That's awesome! What are you doing it on? I wanted to tell you about this recent spike in funding we got that's seemingly going straight into the football program. I think it would make for a great piece on-

ALLY clears her throat.

LIZ: Right, sorry. We're not here to talk about journalism.

HOPE: What are you here for, then?

LIZ: Long story, there's this thing that Bree promised Alex who told Camden who told-

ALLY: Do you want to go to a party with us?

HOPE perks up immediately.

HOPE: A party?!

ALLY: It's at this senior's house. He has a pool.

HOPE: I'd love to go to a party.

LIZ: It's kind of fun! Bree's old friends are always there and it's all these cool people. It's a good time.

HOPE: Do you think they would mind me being a freshman?

LIZ: Well-

ALLY: Just don't say you're a freshman.

HOPE: I can do that.

ALLY: It's on Friday at seven.

HOPE: Oh…

LIZ: What?

HOPE: I don't have a car…or a license, and my mom would never take me to a party.

ALLY: I'm driving. I can pick you up. We were all planning on going together.

LIZ: It'll be really fun.

ALLY: Friday at seven. I'll meet you at your house.

ALLY and LIZ begin to walk away.

HOPE: Wait!

ALLY and LIZ turn around.

HOPE: Can Jaydin come?

JAYDIN: Hope, you don't have to-

ALLY: No.

HOPE: Why not?

ALLY: We already invited you. I don't want to up the freshman count.

LIZ: It's not that big a deal.

JAYDIN: I don't want to go. Also, I'm not a freshman.

HOPE: It's just one more person, Ally. Why can't we bring them?

JAYDIN: I don't-

ALLY: Because I said so!

HOPE: Ally, why are you being so-

LIZ: Both of you! Stop!

ALLY: It's just you, or no one at all, Hope.

ALLY exits, marching off. LIZ follows. JAYDIN looks over at HOPE, who looks angry.

JAYDIN: I didn't want to go, Hope. I don't want to go. I don't need to go.

HOPE: I'm sorry, I don't know why I-. I'm sorry.

JAYDIN: It's okay, just- calm down.

> *HOPE looks off where LIZ and ALLY left.*
> **Blackout**

Scene 10

BREE, LIZ and ALLY all sit in the car. HOPE enters and gets in.
ALLY drives.

LIZ: So! Party night, right guys?

BREE: I'm excited!

HOPE: How far away is it?

ALLY: I don't know, a couple miles.

BREE: Ally, what's up with the sweater?

ALLY: I'm cold.

BREE: It's eighty degrees.

ALLY: I'm still cold.

LIZ: Ally, you're gonna give yourself heatstroke. We're not that far from my place, I could grab a top you can borrow.

ALLY: No, I'm fine.

BREE: Are you sick?

ALLY: I'm fine!

LIZ: You're going to get sick dressed like that. Look at your face, you're already red!

ALLY: Stop! I'm fine! Forgive me for not wanting to go dressed in booty shorts looking like a tease. Unlike *some* people.

BREE: Real subtle.

HOPE: You didn't tell me what to wear! Nobody told me there was a dress code.

ALLY: Sorry, I didn't realize how sleazy you thought people dressed.

BREE: Oh c'mon, Ally.

LIZ: You're being a jerk.

ALLY: I'm just being candid.

HOPE: You're being unfair. I've never been to a high school party, Ally. I've never been to highschool before now! You're so stuck in your little bubble that you treat everyone else like trash! I'm trying to be your *friend.*

ALLY: If it weren't for Writers' Circuit, you'd never even have to try to be my friend.

HOPE purses her lips, fuming. LIZ, slightly panicked, interjects.

LIZ: How about you two breathe for a second, okay? Take a deep breath. This is a fun night. Chill out. For the love of god, stop making things dramatic.

The car is silent.

LIZ: What's everyone excited about? Huh? Fun night! What are you all looking forward to?

Silence

LIZ: Well, I'm excited for the music. I love party music, I can't wait to hear what they pick.

The car stops.

LIZ: Would you look at that, we're here! I can't wait to see what-

JOHN walks in front of the car to the party.

ALLY: Oh god.

LIZ: -music they have.

ALLY: John's here.

BREE: I know.

LIZ: You dated.

BREE: ...I know.

LIZ: Are you going to be okay?

BREE: Of course. I'm over it. I don't care about him. He's history.

ALLY: Are you sure? We can find something else to do.

BREE: No, I'm fine. Let's go.

They all get out of the car.
Blackout

Scene 11

The party. BREE, HOPE, and LIZ all stand together. ALLY stands off, mingling with ENSEMBLE members.

HOPE: This is a lot of people,

LIZ: Don't stress. It's just teenagers.

HOPE: Just...teenagers.

BREE: You're tense. Do you want a drink?

HOPE: Oh, I don't-

BREE steals a cup out of someone else's hand. She mouths thank you. The person rolls their eyes. She holds the cup out to HOPE and nudges her.

HOPE: I'm not drinking someone else's drink.

BREE: Suit yourself!

BREE chugs the cup and exits.

HOPE: She drinks too?

LIZ: She'll be okay.

HOPE: You sure?

LIZ: *(Doubting)* Yes.

BREE returns with 2 cups. She hands one to HOPE.

BREE: I poured it with my own hands.

HOPE: I really appreciate it, Bree, but-

BREE holds the cup out further towards HOPE.

BREE: It's a *party,* Hope, live a little.

HOPE hesitantly takes the cup, and she takes a sip and coughs.

HOPE: That is...not good.

BREE: You'll get used to it! Camden invited me to play beer pong! Go mingle!

BREE runs off.

LIZ: You should...go mingle, I mean. I'm gonna go watch Bree.

LIZ chases after BREE, leaving HOPE behind. HOPE stands awkwardly, still sipping at her drink and puckering with each sip. JOHN approaches her.

JOHN: Hey, lone ranger.

HOPE: Hello?

JOHN: What's a pretty girl like you doing here by yourself.

HOPE: I'm not by myself, my friends took me here, but they left me-

JOHN: By yourself?

HOPE: *(Defeated)* Yeah, I guess.

JOHN: What's your name?

HOPE: I'm Hope.

JOHN: Hope. That's a pretty name.

HOPE: Thanks, my mom gave it to me.

JOHN doesn't laugh.

JOHN: And funny too! The total package.

HOPE: Thanks.

JOHN: You're *real* pretty.

HOPE: Uh- thanks.

JOHN: *(Getting a lot closer)* You've got such nice hair.

HOPE: I-uh-

JOHN: My ex used to have hair almost as-

> *JOHN touches her hair. HOPE steps back.*

JOHN: Silky.

HOPE: Oh, wow.

JOHN: But you are *so* much prettier than her.

HOPE: You're drunk.

JOHN: And you're here.

HOPE: Pardon?

JOHN: You're not a regular at these parties.

HOPE: Yes, I am.

JOHN: Is that right?

HOPE: I go to parties all the time.

JOHN: Right. *(Gesturing to HOPE's cup)* What'cha got there?

HOPE: Uh- vodka.

JOHN: That's beer.

HOPE: That's what I meant.

JOHN: I'm sure. *(Getting closer)* C'mon Hope, no need to be all nervous around me. I'm sure we can get along...well.

> *HOPE takes a big step backward and laughs nervously.*

HOPE: I should go find my friends.

JOHN: They left you. I think they've made their position clear.

> *JOHN steps closer again.*

HOPE: Bree and Liz are probably-

JOHN: Bree Flandel?

HOPE: You know her?

JOHN: Well that's one way to put it.

HOPE: Wait a second, you're the guy from the street.

JOHN: Hm?

HOPE: Bree's ex.

JOHN: She talks about me, does she?

HOPE: She- I'm going to go find her.

> *HOPE starts to leave, and JOHN grabs her by the waist.*

JOHN: She's not worth your time.

HOPE: She's my friend, I need to-

JOHN pulls her in closer to him, HOPE turns to face him.

JOHN: Don't.

HOPE struggles with JOHN and he lets go, she begins to walk away.

JOHN: They're royalty, Hope. And you're only a maid to them.

HOPE turns around.

JOHN: You'll only ever be a maid to them.

HOPE: I'm their *equal.* We're friends.

JOHN: How sure of that are you?

HOPE: Very!

JOHN: What if I told you your friends are not who you think they are.

HOPE: I would call your bluff!

JOHN: And if I told you I had proof?

HOPE: I would tell you to prove it.

JOHN leads HOPE out of the party, and then to his car.

HOPE: Where is it?

JOHN: She left her old phone in my car, she thought she lost it, she got a new one.

HOPE: You have her phone?!

JOHN: Her messages are backed up, I read what she texts to Ally and Liz about you.

HOPE: Then show me the phone!

JOHN: Not out in the open.

JOHN unlocks his car and opens the backseat door and gestures for her to get in. HOPE enters.

JOHN: Look under the seat, on the far side.

JOHN gets in next to her.

JOHN: Deep under the seat.

JOHN looks her up and down. She rises, confused.

HOPE: I can't see anything under there, are you sure it's-

JOHN grabs her and kisses her. HOPE struggles to break free. He does not stop and begins grabbing at her top. HOPE kicks to no avail, but opens the door, falling out of the car. JOHN grabs her and begins to pull at her skirt, she kicks him, gets up and runs out into the road with a torn shirt, smudged lipstick and a crooked skirt. BREE stumbles out of the house.

HOPE: Bree?!

BREE slurs as she speaks

BREE: Hope! I was looking for you. *(Looking at her head to toe)* Who were *you* with?

JOHN chases after HOPE.

BREE: John?

JOHN: *(Pleased) Bree*! Baby! How are you?

BREE processes the information and begins to scream at HOPE.

BREE: John? JOHN?! You were with John?!

HOPE: No, you don't understand, I didn't-

JOHN: Let me go get you your audience.

JOHN waltzes back into the party.

BREE: I was your friend! I invited you here! And what did you do? You screwed my ex-boyfriend?!

HOPE: Bree, listen to me-

BREE: Was that what you wanted this whole time? To hook up with my *ex?*

HOPE: Bree, please!

BREE: You're a slut, Hope. A disgusting, lying, slut!

ALLY AND LIZ run out into the street.

ALLY: There you are!

LIZ: What happened?

ALLY: *(To HOPE)* Who did you do?!

HOPE: I didn't *do* anyone! John tricked me, he-

ALLY: John?! You hooked up with John Wollons?

BREE: You disgusting, worthless, piece of-

LIZ: Hey! Enough!

HOPE looks at BREE pleadingly who stares back at HOPE in anger. After a moment of silence BREE speaks.

BREE: I quit.

ALLY: Quit what?

BREE: I quit Writers' Circuit.

LIZ: Bree, think about what you're doing. You need this for-

BREE: Don't tell me what I need. I need all of you out of my life.

ALLY: Bree! I didn't do anything! This isn't my fault!

HOPE: It's not what it looks like.

BREE: Don't call me.

BREE exits, marching.

ALLY: Bree! Wait.

ALLY turns to HOPE, furious.

ALLY: I knew you were trouble. Are you really *that* desperate?! I hope you're happy, Hope. You just ruined the only good thing I had. You cheating liar! But now you got what you wanted, right? You're out of Writers' Circuit and you're free to write all the poems you want. Hey, maybe you can write a love poem for John.

ALLY gets close to HOPE

ALLY: I will never forgive you. You ruin everything. You're a mistake. I hope you get what you wanted. I hope you get all the friends you want, Hope. *(Screaming)* I hope you feel like this one day. I hope you know what it feels like to get screwed over by someone who doesn't even care.

In tearful anger, ALLY pushes HOPE into the side of JOHN's car. She exits, running. LIZ helps HOPE up and gives her a hug.

HOPE: I didn't do anything with him.

LIZ: I know you didn't.

HOPE: He tried to-

LIZ grabs her house key out of her purse and drags it against the side of JOHN's car.

LIZ: I know.

LIZ hugs HOPE again, and HOPE cries.

Blackout

Scene 12

Physics class. HOPE and CYNTHIA sit at their desks.

HOPE: Hey!

CYNTHIA: *(Unenthused)* Hey.

HOPE: What's up?

CYNTHIA: Waiting for Ms. Roberton to get here.

HOPE: As always! She's got a class to teach.

CYNTHIA: Is missing events not something you do much?

HOPE: Oh… Cynthia, I didn't mean to- I forgot about it and I-

CYNTHIA: Went to a party with Ally Colcone, I know.

HOPE: How did you know I went to a-

CYNTHIA: Jaydin told me.

HOPE: Cynthia, I totally blanked, I'm so sorry.

CYNTHIA: It's fine.

HOPE: If it means anything to you, I didn't have fun.

CYNTHIA: Oh?

HOPE: Everyone was drinking, and Ally was mad at me. My friends left me. Then this guy came up to me and started flirting and he-

CYNTHIA: Hope, if I can be frank with you, I don't really want to talk about a party I wasn't invited or allowed to go to.

HOPE: Cynthia, I'm so sorry. I just-

CYNTHIA: It's okay. I'll get over it. But it hurts now. It's going to hurt now.

HOPE: I feel terrible.

CYNTHIA: There's no need to now. I'll be fine with it later, but please just give me some time to feel this out.

HOPE: I know how I can make you feel better!

CYNTHIA: Hope, I know you mean well but please just listen to me. I just need some time alone.

HOPE: I'll buy you tea at lunch, how about that?

CYNTHIA: Hope! Are you even listening to me? *(Beat.)* Y'know, I think I need a break today. I'm just going to spend my lunch in the library, okay?

HOPE: Are you serious?

CYNTHIA: Yes, I'm serious.

HOPE: Because I didn't come to your show? I think that's a little much, don't you think?

CYNTHIA: No, I don't. You said you were coming. I saved you a seat. I was excited for you to come. I just need some time to be angry.

HOPE: Fine, whatever. Go be angry. I'm sure you'll love everyone comforting you. Well, I'm not coming to *this show* either.

CYNTHIA looks at HOPE, hurt.

CYNTHIA: I need to go to the bathroom, so I-

CYNTHIA takes a breath and exits, holding back tears. HOPE sits in anger for a moment before going wide eyed.

HOPE: Oh god, what have I done.

HOPE wrings her hands for a moment and then puts her head on her desk.

Blackout.

Scene 13

ALLY stands outside of BREE's door. BREE looks worse than before. ALLY knocks on the door.

BREE: Come in.

ALLY enters

ALLY: Hey.

BREE: Hi.

ALLY: How are you doing?

BREE: Could be better. You?

ALLY: Could be better.

BREE: What did you need?

ALLY: I just… I came to talk to you about-

BREE: You said you left something here and you needed it.

ALLY: I just said that, so you'd talk to me.

BREE: You lied?

ALLY: It was important.

BREE: You can lie just because you think it's important?

ALLY: That's not what I'm here to talk about.

BREE: I didn't say we were going to talk. I said you could come get what you needed. If there's nothing you need here, then go.

ALLY: I need you. I want my best friend back.

BREE: Ally, if that's why you're here-

ALLY: Please. I didn't do anything wrong! I wasn't with Hope the whole night!

BREE: Ally, please just go.

ALLY: What about Writers' Circuit? Your college tuition? We were going to major in English and British Literature together!

BREE: I'm sorry, Ally. I just-

ALLY: So, you're just leaving? Leaving Writers' Circuit, leaving Liz, leaving *me.*

BREE: Ally, don't make this harder than it has to be.

ALLY: It does have to be hard! You're all I have, Bree.

BREE: You have Liz.

ALLY: Do I? Since when have Liz and I gotten along?

BREE: Since, when have *we?*

ALLY: Don't say that.

BREE: All you do is talk trash about my friends. Just because I don't call you out on it, doesn't mean I don't feel it.

ALLY: What are you talking about?

BREE: You were mean to Hope when we were friends, you're mean to Liz, you're mean to everyone you meet. When do I get pulled into that? When do you start treating me the way you treat Hope?

ALLY: I would never-

BREE: Stop.

ALLY: I am a good friend. I would never hurt you! I would never-

BREE: I'm quitting Writers' Circuit, Ally.

ALLY: Please, Bree.

BREE: I've made my decision.

ALLY: Why? Why do you have to be so *selfish?*

BREE: Please just go.

ALLY: You were my best friend.

BREE: Ally.

ALLY: What changed, Bree? What happened that made you do this.

BREE: I just- I just don't think we were meant to be friends, Ally. You're self-centered. You're conceited and bitter. You're a terrible friend, Ally. I just don't *like* you.

   Silence. ALLY painfully processes the statement.

ALLY: Well if that's how you feel, then I'll go. I guess I just never knew what sober Bree thought of me, I haven't really met her much at all.

 ALLY exits, storming out of the door and slamming it. BREE stares at her floor and eventually grabs a syringe from under her mattress.

Blackout

<u>End of Act I</u>

Act 2

Scene 1

CYNTHIA stands centerstage, texting HOPE. There is a beat between each text.

CYNTHIA: I'm sorry for the way things went down. *(Beat.)* I mean, we both made mistakes and I don't think it's fair to hold you to yours and not hold myself to mine. *(Beat.)* When you have time, we should talk it out. Face to face. *(Beat.)*

The lights dim.

O/S BOY 1: Who's coming to the Halloween party?

O/S GIRL 1: My Dorothy costume is so cute! I look just like Judy Garland!

O/S BOY 2: Is there a cover charge?

O/S GIRL 2: I'm so sad, I have to take my niece trick or treating, I don't want to miss the party.

O/S BOY 1: Happy Halloween!

The lights rise up on CYNTHIA, in a different outfit. She still texts.

CYNTHIA: Happy Halloween. *(Beat.)* You haven't messaged me since last week. *(Beat.)* Jaydin and I are hanging out after school if you want to come. *(Beat.)* I'm worried about you.

The lights dim

O/S BOY 1: I'm still hungover from this weekend.

O/S GIRL 1: Halloween is my favorite holiday *ever.*

O/S BOY 2: I'm still buzzed.

O/S GIRL 2: Please stop tagging me in the party pictures!

O/S BOY 1: I'm getting no work done today.

The lights rise on CYNTHIA in a different outfit. She still texts.

CYNTHIA: If you want you could get coffee with Jaydin and I. *(Beat.)* Hope, please. *(Beat.)* Just message me back! *(Beat.)* If you're mad we can talk it out. *(Beat.)* I miss you.

Lights rise on HOPE. HOPE picks up her phone, sighs, and puts it down. When HOPE puts the phone down, the light on CYNTHIA blacks out. YOUNG HOPE stands center stage, and HOPE paces beside her.

YOUNG HOPE: I can't wait for high school. I can't wait to have friends and go to parties and be in love. I can't wait to be a grown up and go to prom and get straight A's.

HOPE stops pacing and sinks down to sit beside her bed

YOUNG HOPE: Everything will be absolutely perfect. I'll be so, so, so- happy!

HOPE throws her head into her hands. YOUNG HOPE fades out and exits. CYNTHIA appears, texting HOPE.

CYNTHIA: Just checking in, hoping you're alright.

HOPE exclaims in anger, and angrily throws her phone across the room. CYNTHIA's light goes out.

HOPE: *(in a fit of anger)* Stop messaging me! Stop asking me questions! Just stop talking to me! Everyone just stop talking to me, stop pretending to be my friend, I don't care anymore.

She kicks her bed

HOPE: I-

She kicks

HOPE: Don't-

She kicks again

HOPE: Care!

She kicks a third time, this time she begins to cry. She starts to sit down beside her bed again, but her phone rings. A light appears on LIZ, on her phone on the other side of the stage. HOPE takes a deep breath before walking over to her phone. She hesitates over it before picking it up.

HOPE: Please don't be broken. Please don't be broken. Please don't be-

She picks up her phone

HOPE: Thank god. *(beat.)* Liz? Why would Liz call me-?

HOPE answers the phone

LIZ: Hope?

HOPE: Liz?

LIZ: Hey, I was just thinking about you. How have you been?

HOPE: How have *you* been?

LIZ: I've been fine. Don't deflect.

HOPE: I'm glad you're fine! Anything exciting going on?

LIZ: *Hope.* How are you.

HOPE: I'm whatever- y'know. I'm me.

LIZ: Hope...

HOPE: I'm *fine.*

LIZ: Fine, alright. Well, *fine,* if you'd like to come over I can pick you up.

HOPE: I don't want to intrude-

LIZ: I'm inviting you. Please?

HOPE: When will you be here?

LIZ: I'm already on my way.
> *HOPE grabs her bag and exits.*

Blackout

Scene 2

A coffee shop. CYNTHIA and JAYDIN sit together.

CYNTHIA: I thought she would've answered by now. I'm really getting worried.

JAYDIN: Well, she's been at school this whole time, y'know. She's not dead.

CYNTHIA: I know that, I just-

JAYDIN: I get it. This is all really strange. It's not even Thanksgiving break yet, she'll have time to change and grow and work past all of this.

CYNTHIA: But the thing is, I don't want her to change all the way. I want the her I met the first day of school.

JAYDIN: You've only known her for two months, the way she was at the beginning of school could've just been a front.

CYNTHIA: No... she seemed so genuine, Jaydin. She was real and raw. It wasn't a front.

JAYDIN: You don't know that.

CYNTHIA: But I feel it.

JAYDIN: Even then, people change. She's a freshman. All freshman *do* is change.

CYNTHIA: Why would she? She was happy and intelligent.

JAYDIN: She's still intelligent, Cynthia. I'm in journalism with her. And high school is hard, she's probably just struggling.

CYNTHIA: I know, I know. I just think that she's let all of her friends drag her down.

JAYDIN: Which friends?

CYNTHIA: Her writers' circuit group- Ally Colcone and-

JAYDIN: Say no more.

CYNTHIA: You know her?

JAYDIN: She was my partner in Chemistry.

CYNTHIA: She was hanging with Hope all the time.

JAYDIN: You think that's why she's in a rough place right now?

CYNTHIA: I mean, not totally. I probably threw her off the edge when I blew up at her.

JAYDIN: You had a right to be angry.

CYNTHIA: I know but I shouldn't have snapped at-

JAYDIN: Stop it.

CYNTHIA: But I-

JAYDIN: Seriously. Knock it off. Hope's mental state does not revolve around you, or Ally Colcone, now that I think about it.

CYNTHIA: What do you mean?

JAYDIN: Ally isn't the sole proprietor of Hope's social life. She has other friends. It's probably just a mix of things.

CYNTHIA: But I still want to know what's going on with her. I want to be able to help.

JAYDIN: I can message Liz for you, if you want.

CYNTHIA: Do you think she'd know?

JAYDIN: I think she's the only person you could bet on at this point. It's worth a shot.

CYNTHIA: Okay then.

JAYDIN: I'll message her on Social Scroll today. See if she knows why Hope's been avoiding you.

CYNTHIA: I owe you one.

Blackout

Scene 3

*LIZ's room. HOPE sits on a chair and LIZ sits on her bed.
Textbooks clutter a desk.*

LIZ: Nothing really. Bree and I've talked on and off, but I've avoided Ally's texts.

HOPE: Ally's texted you?

LIZ: Why wouldn't she?

HOPE: Because she has a vendetta against us now.

LIZ: She's angry at you. She still wants Bree and I to be friends with her.

HOPE: Oh.

LIZ: It's nothing against you. I think she's just in a rough place.

HOPE: Why are you avoiding her texts?

LIZ: As dumb as it is, I'm not sure I'm ready to go back into her rough place. She's never very nice to me anyway. I think she'd manage well without me.

HOPE: That's not dumb, and that's her loss.

LIZ: What about you? How've you been? And if you say fine I'm going to throw something.

HOPE: Things- are just. I don't know what to do. I feel- dirty.

LIZ: Why?

HOPE: The whole mess with John. I just- what if I hadn't gotten out.

LIZ: But you did. You're safe.

HOPE: I know that... it just still makes me feel dirty. When the lights go out it's like I still feel him. I feel sick every time I see him in the hall. I've washed my face over and over but all I can picture is his mouth on mine.

HOPE wrings her hands and LIZ looks at her with intense empathy.

LIZ: Oh, Hope.

HOPE: And I know I'm lucky. It could've been so much worse and-

LIZ: You're allowed to feel like that. What he did was- despicable.

HOPE looks at LIZ and LIZ smiles at her

LIZ: He can't hurt you anymore.

HOPE: He still goes to our school and he-

LIZ: I won't let him.

HOPE moves to LIZ's bed and sits next to LIZ. LIZ puts her arm around HOPE.

LIZ: You're safe.

A moment passes with the two girls on the bed, HOPE breaks the silence, changing the subject.

HOPE: I thought you were taking Algebra.

LIZ: I am.

HOPE: What's with the Calculus textbooks?

HOPE walks to the desk and shows LIZ an AP Calculus textbook

LIZ: Oh. I'm teaching myself Calculus.

HOPE: You're teaching yourself... Calculus? How? Why?!

LIZ: Nova Hills doesn't offer a fully AP schedule, and I like writing more. I couldn't fit a full advanced writing and advanced math track in my schedule, so I had to sacrifice one of them.

HOPE: Couldn't you have done summer school or something?

LIZ: I tutor the kids at the middle school in the summer, and the workload would be too strenuous for anyone.

HOPE: That sucks, Liz, I'm sorry.

LIZ: It's fine, I manage. I've had to pick one or the other for years, it's nothing new. There's nothing for writers and mathematicians - at least not here.

HOPE: So, you're just going to abandon math?

LIZ: Oh god no, I'm teaching myself as much as possible now so that I'm ready for college. That way I can double major, or at least have an even choice.

HOPE: That's amazing. I hate math, I couldn't imagine doing it every day.

LIZ: Why does everyone say that!? It's not as bad as everyone makes it out to be!

HOPE: *(Lighthearted)* Maybe for you!

HOPE freezes, lights go up on JAYDIN, messaging LIZ. LIZ pulls out her phone to read their message.

JAYDIN: Hey Liz! It's Jaydin from Journalism. We're in a group project together?

LIZ: Hey, Jaydin! What's up?

JAYDIN: I was talking to my friend and we're just worried about Hope.

LIZ: Which friend?

JAYDIN: Cynthia LaBelle?

LIZ: Oh, okay!

JAYDIN: Yeah, Hope hasn't responded to any of Cynthia's messages in weeks, and she worried, and looking at everything, I think I'm a little worried too.

LIZ: I'll talk to her about it.

JAYDIN: I appreciate it so much.

LIZ: No problem!

JAYDIN fades and exits. HOPE unfreezes

HOPE: Who ya texting?

LIZ: Jaydin - from Journalism.

HOPE: Oh, I love them!

LIZ: Me too. *(beat.)* Hey, Hope?

HOPE: Yeah?

LIZ: Are you friends with Cynthia LaBelle?

HOPE gets visibly uncomfortable

HOPE: Kind of, yeah.

LIZ: Do you guys talk much?

HOPE: I don't think I want to get into it.

LIZ: Sorry, I didn't realize it was-

HOPE: No, no, it's nothing, you're fine.

There is an awkward silence for a moment.

HOPE: I just kind of stopped talking to her after the party.

LIZ: Why?

HOPE: We got in a fight and I'm not really sure- I don't know.

LIZ: What do you mean?

HOPE: I just don't know.

LIZ: Hope, please, she's worried about you.

HOPE: She put you up to asking me?!

LIZ: Jaydin and her were just wanting to know if you were-

HOPE: Oh my god, I didn't answer her texts because I don't want to deal with her right now! I'm so tired of everyone making me talk-

LIZ: If this is about me saying you weren't fine, I-

HOPE: I don't know? Okay. I don't know what this is about I'm just so frustrated.

LIZ: You don't have to be-

HOPE: Just- just let me be, right now okay. I'm gonna call my mom to pick me up.

LIZ: Hope, I didn't mean to-

HOPE: I'm not- I'm not mad. I'm just… I think I'm just overwhelmed right now.

LIZ: Is there anything I can do?

HOPE: Right now, I just need to be alone.

LIZ: Okay.

HOPE grabs her bag and leaves

Blackout

Scene 4

Nova Hills High School hallway. Students walk the halls. A very high BREE leans against a locker, spaced out.

O/S GIRL 1: Does anyone want to ditch third hour with me?

O/S BOY 1: I was up so late finishing my biology paper, KMS.

O/S GIRL 2: Look at this post from Nova Hills' ConfessMe page!

O/S BOY 2: I'll skip with you.

O/S GIRL 1: @ClaireBoregard, wishing you were in my lunch period

As the offstage students speak, ALLY enters, opening her locker.

O/S BOY 1: I saw that ConfessMe post, kinda weird TBH.

O/S GIRL 2: I lost my Chemistry book, Ms. Williams is going to kill me.

ALLY closes her locker loudly, making the students stop. She sees BREE and walks over to her.

ALLY: Bree! Long time no see!

BREE speaks slowly. She seems spaced out.

BREE: Yeah.

ALLY: How have you been?

BREE flashes ALLY a half-hearted thumbs up.

ALLY: Uh, great! Look I was thinking about our fight and I think if we just stopped and thought about it, and we both really looked at *why* we said what we said, I think we could really work past this.

BREE: What?

ALLY: I said that if we really talked this out, we could be friends again.

BREE stares at ALLY

BREE: You try too hard.

ALLY: I try because I care.

BREE: Why?

ALLY: Because you mean so much to me, and I don't want to lose you. I help you! We make each other better.

BREE: You… don't help me.

ALLY: I can! I can help you with your… y'know… *problem.*

BREE: What *problem*?

ALLY mimics smoking a cigarette. BREE laughs.

BREE: I don't need you.

ALLY: Well, then I don't have to help you. I just want to be-

BREE: Ally, I don't want to be friends with you. You're… too much.

BREE tries to smile but ends up just walking away.

ALLY: *(Calling)* Bree! Please!

Bree exits. HOPE walks by, and ALLY grabs her arm and pulls her over.

HOPE: Ally?

ALLY: Hope, I've been meaning to talk to you.

HOPE: Okay?

ALLY: I'm sorry for the party.

HOPE: No, it's okay, it was a rough night for everyone.

ALLY: I shouldn't have pushed you and yelled at you.

HOPE: Thank you.

ALLY: I just hope it doesn't hurt our friendship.

HOPE: Oh…

ALLY: I was wondering if you wanted to maybe hang out after school.

HOPE: Ally… I was thinking about things and I'm not totally sure I'm ready to hang out again.

ALLY: Because I pushed you?

HOPE: Lots of things. I'm not saying never I just… maybe we should distance ourselves for a while.

ALLY: Oh… okay.

HOPE: I'm sorry, I'm just not ready to-

ALLY: No, no it's totally okay.

HOPE: See you around!

ALLY: You too.

Hope exits. ALLY, hurt and frustrated, begins to type on her phone. The offstage students walk by, all reading on their phones. ALLY speaks, and the students commentate. They seem to almost fight for the audience's attention.

ALLY: I'm never good enough for anyone. I don't understand why everyone hates me so much.

I try so hard to be perfect. I try so hard to be fun, and smart, and cool. It's never enough. It's never enough for anyone.

Maybe it's just time to stop trying with them. I'm just not sure I'm ready for that yet.

I'll give it one more try. I'll give them one more chance.

O/S GIRL 1: Look at the new post on the Nova Hills' ConfessMe page.

O/S BOY 1: This is? Depressing.

O/S GIRL 2: Jeez, who is this person?

O/S BOY 2: I kinda feel bad for them.

O/S GIRL 1: Not to be mean, but I kinda feel bad for their friends. They kinda seem… like a lot.

O/S BOY 1: Honestly, they need to chill out and take a breath…

ALLY puts her phone down; the students go silent.
Blackout.

Scene 5

HOPE enters her journalism classroom. The students are there. Before HOPE sits down, PIERRE calls her over.

PIERRE: Hope, can I have a word?

HOPE walks over to PIERRE

PIERRE: Hope, Cynthia LaBelle asked me very kindly if I'd allow you two to talk in the hallway.

HOPE: I'd rather not.

PIERRE: I know, but I think it would be best if you'd take a moment to work something out with her.

HOPE: She's not even in this class.

PIERRE: I know. *(Pause.)* She's in the hallway.

HOPE: I…

PIERRE looks at HOPE.

HOPE: Ok.

HOPE exits the classroom and into the hallway. CYNTHIA immediately goes to greet her.

CYNTHIA: Hope!

HOPE: I really don't want to-

CYNTHIA: I know you don't want to talk. I get that. I'm sorry if I upset you, I was so caught up in myself that I-

HOPE: Don't do that.

CYNTHIA: Do what?

HOPE: Make excuses for me.

CYNTHIA: I'm just trying to make you understand that I'm not mad at you.

HOPE: Ok.

CYNTHIA: And that I want to fix things. Hope, I'm so worried about you. You don't talk to me in physics, you don't answer my texts. I get that I made you mad, but it's not fair for you to completely ghost me.

HOPE: I'm sorry.

CYNTHIA: Hope, *please.* I thought I was being nice and being a good friend. You're making me feel like you don't want to be friends, and that I'm just not good enough for you.

HOPE spikes her head up, and immediately begins to fiddle with her hands.

HOPE: I didn't mean to make you feel like that.

CYNTHIA: I know you didn't, it's just how I felt.

HOPE: I should've responded to you. I was just- actually, I don't know. I was just angry.

CYNTHIA: And you have a right to be-

HOPE: No, I don't. I didn't come to your show, and I'm sorry. I was in the wrong.

CYNTHIA: Well, I was too-

HOPE: No. You don't have to say sorry and all. I do.

CYNTHIA: I'm just glad you're talking to me again.

HOPE: I'm sorry I wasn't a good friend.

CYNTHIA: You don't have to apologize.

HOPE: You deserve an apology.

CYNTHIA smiles and gives HOPE a hug.

HOPE: I will never ditch you for a stupid party ever again.

They laugh.

CYNTHIA: Hey, what did you mean when you said that you didn't have fun at the party.

HOPE: Oh… It's a long story.

CYNTHIA: I'm willing to listen.

HOPE: It was just… do you know John Wollons?

CYNTHIA: I'm aware of him, yeah.

HOPE: He, well he tried to… uh-

CYNTHIA stares at HOPE, fearful of what she's going to say.

HOPE: He got me in his car and he wanted to- I mean I didn't want to- and I didn't but Bree thought I did and I-

HOPE wrings her hands, and CYNTHIA grabs her and hugs her tightly.

CYNTHIA: I'm so sorry, Hope.

HOPE: It's fine, I'm fine.

CYNTHIA: It's okay if you're not.

CYNTHIA continues to hug HOPE. There is a moment of silence.

HOPE: I'm not.

Blackout

Scene 6

BREE sits on the floor of the hallway, now empty, texting. She looks absolutely terrible.

BREE: Can you come meet me in the east wing hallway. Near the library?

A light lights up LIZ, responding to BREE's text

LIZ: I'm in class.

BREE: Which class?

LIZ: English.

BREE: You're good at English.

LIZ: I know, I'd like to stay good at English.

BREE: Liz, please.

LIZ: Okay, I'm coming.

LIZ enters. BREE looks up at her.

LIZ: Are you okay?

BREE: No.

LIZ: Can you stand up?

BREE: I'm fine here.

LIZ: What's up?

BREE pats the floor, inviting LIZ to sit. LIZ sits down.

BREE: I can't do this anymore.

LIZ: Do what.

BREE: This.

LIZ: School? Writers' Circuit? Skipping class, I hope it's skipping class because you really should-

BREE: This isn't a joke, Liz.

LIZ: Sorry.

BREE: It's fine.

(Beat.)

LIZ: What's going on?

BREE: I woke up on the sidewalk this morning.

LIZ: In front of your house?

BREE: I don't know how I got there.

LIZ: Bree, you've got to stop drinking. It's getting-

BREE: I wasn't drunk.

LIZ: What?

BREE: When you came over to my house and asked if I was doing… taking more than weed, I told you no, but-

LIZ: Bree…

BREE: I thought I had things under control but I just-

LIZ: Bree…

BREE: Stop saying that.

LIZ: What do you want me to say? How am I supposed to feel, Bree?

BREE: I want you to tell me that I'll be okay.

LIZ: When? Bree, heroin is serious stuff are you-

BREE: I'm going to stop. That's why I told you.

LIZ: Bree...

BREE: I need a place to stay. I'm not safe at my house anymore.

LIZ: Why?

BREE: I can't get home without running into my dealer. I need to stay with you for a bit.

LIZ: Bree, you need to see a doctor.

BREE: I can do it alone.

LIZ: No.

BREE: Fine, then I'll have you and Hope.

LIZ: I don't know how to help you get off of heroin, Bree. I'm a teenager. I've never even smoked weed. You need to go to rehab or something.

BREE: Liz, I'm not going to rehab.

LIZ: Do you realize how addictive that stuff is?

BREE: No, actually. If only I was coming to you asking for help to break an addiction.

LIZ: This really isn't the time or place for your bull, Bree. You need help.

BREE: That's why I came to you.

LIZ: You need a doctor, or a specialist, or *somebody*. Jeez, Bree. I can't keep you away from that. I'm sorry. I'll take you to an inpatient place, I'll drive you there myself, just please-

BREE: No! You don't understand!

ALLY walks by and sees BREE and LIZ. She walks over to them.

ALLY: I thought you weren't talking anymore.

BREE: I thought I told you I didn't want to talk.

ALLY: I thought you told Liz the same thing.

LIZ: Ally, I-

ALLY: Liz, you told me our group just wasn't working out.

LIZ: I just- I didn't want to hurt your feelings.

ALLY: Well, thank you so much, because I feel really great now.

LIZ: I'm sorry, Ally, I just-

ALLY: Just what? Just thought I bring you down, you just wanted a better friend group, just thought I'd be better off dead.

BREE: Nobody said that.

ALLY: Maybe not to my face.

LIZ: We're not trash talking you.

ALLY: Because you've never lied to me before.

LIZ: Look, Ally. I'm sorry that I lied to you. I'm not angry or against you. I just think that we weren't a compatible friendship.

ALLY: We've been friends for years.

LIZ: You've talked down to me for years, and made fun of me, and treated me like I wasn't even there!

ALLY: I'm sorry I made you feel that way. I think I just thought that if I did that, I would feel cool.

LIZ: Thank you for apologizing, Ally. I really appreciate it, but things- I'm sorry.

ALLY: I don't understand.

LIZ: It's just… I'm sorry, Ally.

ALLY: It's fine. I get it.

LIZ: I think you're great, I just-

ALLY: Really, it's fine.

ALLY walks out, and LIZ watches her leave.

Blackout

Scene 7

On a dark stage, a figure stands in the back. Phone notification noises begin sounding off.

O/S GIRL 1: That ConfessMe person posted again.

O/S BOY 1: It's like 3 am, why are my notifications going nuts?

O/S GIRL 2: This is really dark.

O/S BOY 2: Who wrote this?

The lights shine on the on-stage actors as they speak, reading off of their phones.

LIZ: I'm sorry I was never good enough for you

BREE: Everyone hates me

HOPE: And I didn't know why

CYNTHIA: But now, I think I do

More panicked.

O/S GIRL 1: The ConfessMe girl is Ally Colcone, she just posted on Social Scroll.

O/S BOY 1: Is she okay?

CYNTHIA: There's something on her page.

BREE: It's a note.

HOPE: She just posted a note.

JAYDIN: I guess this is where it ends.

LIZ picks up her phone, trying to call ALLY.

LIZ: Ally?! Pick up, please.

O/S GIRL 2: Very funny.

ALL: It's not a joke.

HOPE: Who saw her last?

BREE: Is she home alone?

CYNTHIA: Did anyone call the police?

ALL: Does anyone have her mom's number?

The lights blackout, and the cast exits. Lights rise on the figure in the back, ALLY.

ALLY: I'm sorry.

ALLY steps back out of the light.

Blackout

Scene 8

Journalism class. WAVERLY stands in the front of the classroom, speaking. It is solemn.

WAVERLY: I think we should do an editorial on suicide prevention, alert the school and community about the memorial service. I don't think the paper should dwell on it too much.

PIERRE: Is that all?

WAVERLY: I don't know what else to pitch. I don't think there's anything Warrior Weekly can fix. We just have to do the best we can to stay sensitive.

PIERRE: Thank you, Waverly.

WAVERLY sits down, PIERRE addresses the class.

PIERRE: With that, I'm just calling today a free day. Work on what you can with your groups. Take all the time you need.

JAYDIN, LIZ, and HOPE, all sit together silently. HOPE and LIZ say nothing, JAYDIN attempts to start conversation.

JAYDIN: I think we could work on an editorial style piece, but it's entirely fiction. Like our teachers are werewolves and- *(beat.)* I'm so sorry, guys.

The girls don't respond. There is a long moment of silence.

HOPE: Did you know?

LIZ: I thought she was just angry at the world. Or me. Or both. I didn't know she was… how could I have known she was? Did you?

HOPE: Not at all.

LIZ: I told her I didn't want to be friends anymore. I feel so guilty.

HOPE: Me too.

There is more silence. LIZ's phone beeps, BREE appears, texting LIZ.

BREE: Hey.

LIZ: Hey.

BREE: How are you?

LIZ: I don't know. You?

BREE: Guilty.

LIZ: Me too.

BREE: I had three different opportunities to tell her we could be friends.

LIZ: Three?

BREE: She came over to my house, and then stopped me in the hall. And then with you. Out of all those times I never once told her that-

LIZ: I know.

BREE: Do you hate me?

LIZ: Why would I?

BREE: Because I killed Ally.

LIZ: Oh my god, you didn't kill her!

BREE: If I had been nicer...

LIZ: I wasn't nice either. Neither was Hope.

BREE: But I was the worst to her.

LIZ: Can we not compete about this? I really don't want to compete with this.

BREE: Does Hope hate me?

LIZ: No. Do you hate you?

BREE: I don't know.

LIZ: Come over.

BREE: I'm not at school.

LIZ: I mean after. How about you, me and Hope all be together.

BREE: I don't think you and Hope need to see me right now.

LIZ: Please.

BREE: You promise you don't hate me?

LIZ: Not at all.

BREE: Ok.

LIZ puts down her phone.

Blackout

Scene 9

LIZ's house. HOPE, BREE, and LIZ all sit. No one sits in the chair ALLY sat in when they met there before. There is heavy silence. After a moment, BREE speaks up.

BREE: Last time we were all here, Ally was too.

HOPE: I should've known.

LIZ: I just thought she was pessimistic.

BREE: I feel so stupid.

HOPE: Do you think she tried to tell you?

LIZ: I- I don't really know any more. I'm just really confused. Nothing makes sense to me.

BREE: She always said I was all she had, but I thought it was just her being dramatic.

HOPE: I know that she's her own person, but I can't shake the feeling like I killed her.

BREE: You didn't kill her, Hope. I'm the one who did.

HOPE: That's not true.

BREE: A couple days after the party, Ally came to my house. She said she wanted to be friends and that she needed me. I told her no, and we got in a huge fight. She said she didn't know what the sober me thought of her.

LIZ: It's not your fault.
BREE chokes up

BREE: And now that I look back, every time I was with her this year, I've never been sober. I don't even know what sober me thinks about her. I don't even know the sober me.

LIZ: Oh, Bree…

HOPE: I told her I wanted to take a break from her.

LIZ: We all did. We all left.

BREE: I let her down the hardest.

LIZ: Can we *please* not compete, Bree.

HOPE: I just wish I could apologize to her. I'd tell her that I'm sorry for breaking off from her.

>   *There is a moment of silence again. LIZ collects her thoughts.*

LIZ: I don't.

HOPE: What?

LIZ: I wouldn't apologize. I was nice, but I don't have to worship her. It's not my fault that I needed to get away.

>   *LIZ freezes, rethinking her statement.*

LIZ: It's not my fault if I needed to get away.

HOPE: I guess you're right… it just still feels like it's my fault.

LIZ: I know.

>   *There is more silence*

HOPE: I don't even know how I'm going to get through the memorial service.

LIZ: I don't want to go anymore, to be honest.

BREE: Why not?

LIZ: Her family didn't like me, I don't think they'd want me there.

HOPE: You should still go.

LIZ: I will. I need the closure. I just really don't want to.

HOPE: I'm sorry.

LIZ: No, it's fine.

BREE: I'm not going.

HOPE and LIZ both turn to BREE in surprise

LIZ: Why not?

BREE: I can't go. I can't stand there and look at her body. I don't want to listen to her family talk about her. I can't do it. I couldn't do that sober, and I don't think going to her funeral high will bode well for my conscience.

HOPE: Bree, you need to get help.

BREE: No, I don't. I'm fine.

HOPE: Bree-

LIZ: It's what Ally would've wanted.

BREE: Don't guilt trip me.

LIZ: I'm not trying to guilt trip you.

HOPE: Bree, please.

BREE: I've got it under control. Just stay out of it.

LIZ: You asked me for help!

BREE: And you said no!

HOPE: Wait what?

LIZ: I'm not a doctor, I can't cure you of this kind of stuff, Bree. I can help you where I can, but I don't know how to help a heroin addict.

HOPE: Wait, *heroin*?!

LIZ: I'm sorry, I forgot you didn't-

HOPE: Bree, what?!

BREE: I really don't appreciate you spilling my secrets to people, Liz.

LIZ: Bree, this is already hard enough, please don't fight with me.

BREE: Then stop pushing me to go to rehab.

LIZ: I'm trying to keep you safe.

BREE: I'm trying to keep me happy.

LIZ: Do you even hear yourself?

HOPE: Bree, I know this is hard but-

BREE: No! I've already lost Ally. I don't want to go to some rehab place and suffer. Let me grieve my friend.

The conversation escalates into a full-fledged fight. They scream at each other. HOPE sits in her chair, uncomfortable.

LIZ: I'm grieving too, Bree! But now I have to worry about if you'll be okay too! You're not making this any easier for me!

BREE: Wow! I'm so sorry I am such a burden to you.

LIZ: I'm trying to *help*.

BREE: Well you're not doing much.

LIZ: I am in just as much pain as you are. She was my friend too.

BREE: You're the one who said you wouldn't apologize to Ally.

LIZ: I'm so sorry that I won't say that Ally was perfect because she's dead. I guess I'm not in the habit of lying to myself.

BREE: What is that supposed to mean?

LIZ: Do you think you being high all the time helps anyone? It doesn't even help you, Bree. Look at you! You're dying.

BREE: It's not your life!

LIZ: And Ally wasn't your life either, but it still hurts that she's dead.

>   *LIZ begins to tear up as she yells.*

LIZ: I am *watching* you kill yourself, Bree.

>   *LIZ quiets down, to a much quieter tone.*

LIZ: I'm not ready to lose you.

>   *BREE and LIZ both stare at each other. BREE speaks quietly.*

BREE: I'll be okay. I can do this on my own.

>   *LIZ cries more as she shakes her head.*

LIZ: You're dying. You're so sick, Bree. Every time I tell you goodbye, I'm worried it'll be the last time.

BREE: Liz-

LIZ: No.

LIZ chokes back full sobs. BREE watches her, processing.

LIZ: If you don't get help, you are going to make me watch you die.

BREE and LIZ stare at each other again. LIZ looks at BREE, and mutters, barely audibly

LIZ: Please.

BREE breaks down, and HOPE finally gets up from her chair to put her arms around BREE. LIZ does the same.

BREE: I don't want to die.

They hug.

Blackout

Scene 10

December. The lunchroom. Garland and snowflake decor line the cafeteria. JAYDIN, LIZ, and HOPE all sit together, talking about their project.

JAYDIN: Well, I was thinking an evil snowman who wants to ruin Christmas.

HOPE: It's supposed to be non-fiction.

JAYDIN: Do you doubt the existence of evil snowmen? Foolish move.

HOPE, LIZ, and JAYDIN laugh.

LIZ: Are you sad that you couldn't do Writers' Circuit?

HOPE: I'm a freshman, I could always do it next year.

JAYDIN: Cynthia and I are still bummed about missing it.

HOPE: Cynthia writes?

JAYDIN: She wants to try it out. We should team up next year!

LIZ: Well, minus one. Bree will be back by then.

JAYDIN: How is she doing?

LIZ: I got a letter last week. She's doing really well. I'm proud of her.

CYNTHIA enters, putting her lunch tray down at the table.

CYNTHIA: Hey guys!

LIZ: Hey!

HOPE: Which one of us is the minus one?

JAYDIN: You.

HOPE: Fight me.

CYNTHIA: What are you guys talking about?

JAYDIN: Writers' Circuit. We could all team up next year, but we wouldn't be able to have all five of us.

CYNTHIA: Wait, are you guys still down to do the Circuit?

HOPE: Yeah, I just lost my group.

LIZ: Me too.

CYNTHIA: You know they aren't due until February, right?

HOPE: I thought they were due in December.

CYNTHIA: Nope, there's still another two months.

JAYDIN: It would be really hard to write a Novella in two months.

HOPE: I work best under pressure.

LIZ: I'm sure I could manage.

They all smile at each other

CYNTHIA: If we did it, what would it even be about?

JAYDIN: Evil snowmen!

HOPE: No!

LIZ: How about a mathematician who finds themself in space?

CYNTHIA: No.

HOPE: What about a future divided between the rich and poor and a revolution that-

JAYDIN: That's already a thing.

LIZ: Non-fiction?

JAYDIN: Ew.

LIZ: What about realistic fiction?

CYNTHIA: I'm all for that.

JAYDIN: No evil snowmen?

LIZ shakes her head and lightly laughs

HOPE: Or mermaids?

LIZ: Nope.

CYNTHIA: Just people. Just a story about people.

HOPE opens her mouth to speak, but JOHN walks by. He walks towards the table.

JOHN: Hope, can I talk to you?

HOPE stares at him and wrings her hands.

LIZ: No, you cannot.

JOHN: Luckily, I wasn't talking to you.

LIZ: Luckily, I don't give a-

JOHN: Hey, watch your mouth.

CYNTHIA: Don't tell her what to do.

LIZ: What do you want?

JOHN: I need to talk to Hope.

JAYDIN: Whatever you need to say to Hope, you can say to us.

JOHN: I need to talk to Hope, *alone.*

JAYDIN: Not gonna happen.

JOHN gets closer to HOPE to tell her something, LIZ pushes him away from her. JOHN, frustrated, talks to HOPE directly instead of acknowledging anyone else.

JOHN: I saw you talking to one of the guidance counselors the other day after the whole "Speak your voice" assembly, and I wanted to ask you not to say anything about me. It's been months, and I have scholarships I need to keep.

LIZ: You don't have to talk to-

HOPE: You're asking me to not tell anyone, so you can get a scholarship?

JOHN: I *need* the money to go to a good school.

HOPE stares at him in shock and anger

HOPE: Sorry.

JOHN: Hope, please, I didn't even really hurt you-

LIZ gets in his face

LIZ: I am going to do everything in my power to make sure you learn your lesson, and you won't be learning it in a "good school".

JOHN gets angry, he gets really close to HOPE's face again

JOHN: Fine, then. You and your friends can run and tell everyone your little story. I'll watch it blow up in your face.

JOHN storms off angrily

CYNTHIA: Hope, are you okay?

HOPE looks off where JOHN left

HOPE: I think I have an idea for our story.

They all smile.
Blackout
End of Act II
End of Show

www.ingramcontent.com/pod-product-compliance
Lightning Source LLC
Chambersburg PA
CBHW070638130626
46555CB00006B/2593